P9-DDH-824

3 1255 00251 4829

Date Due

DEC 1 0 2007			
FEB 1 2 2008			
AUG 5 2008			
SEP 1 0 2008			
DEC 0 8 2008			
APR 1 6 2009			

BRODART, CO.   Cat. No. 23-233-003   Printed in U.S.A.

BAKER & TAYLOR

TANA HOBAN

I Read Symbols

Greenwillow Books
New York

This one
is especially
for
Jane Schick

Greenwillow Books, a division of
William Morrow & Company, Inc.,
1350 Avenue of the Americas,
New York, NY 10019.
Printed in the
United States of America

10 9 8

Library of Congress
Cataloging in Publication Data
Hoban, Tana.
I read symbols.
Summary: Introduces signs
and symbols frequently
seen along the highway.
1. Traffic signs and signals
—Juvenile literature.
2. Signs and sign-boards—
Juvenile literature.
[1. Traffic signs and signals.
2. Signs and signboards.
3. Signs and symbols]
I. Title.
TE228.H633 1983
001.56   83-1481
ISBN 0-688-02331-2
ISBN 0-688-02332-0 (lib. bdg.)

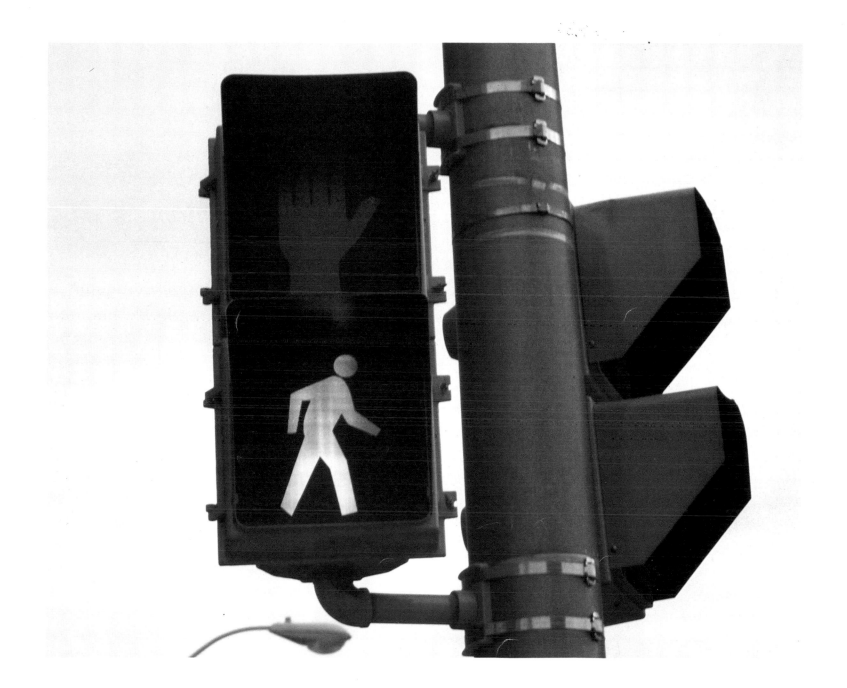

DEPT OF TRAFFIC

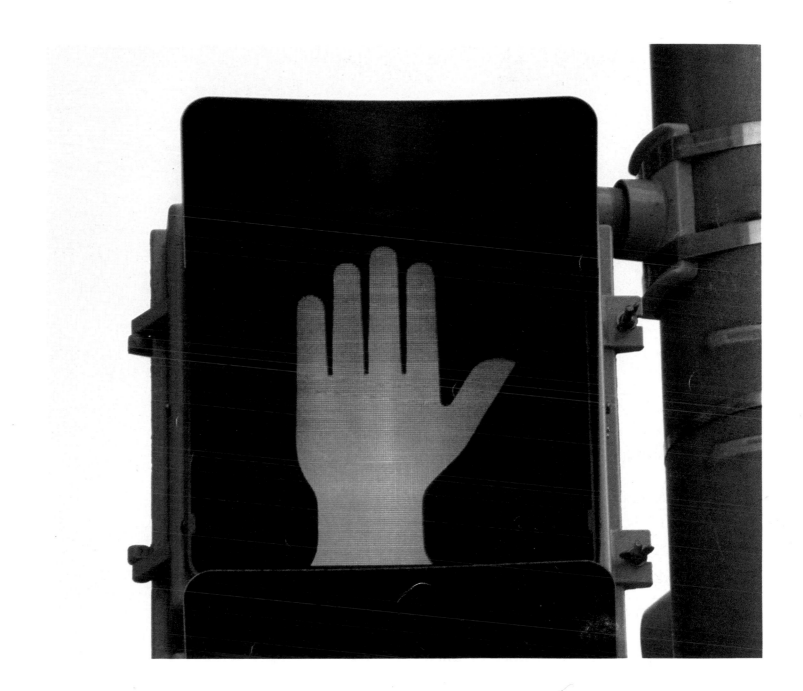

What the Symbols Say

Walk →

Bus stop ahead →

Winding road →

Go left →

Ladies →

Deer crossing →

Go right →

Men →

Trail →

Traffic signal ahead →

Workers ahead →

No left turn →

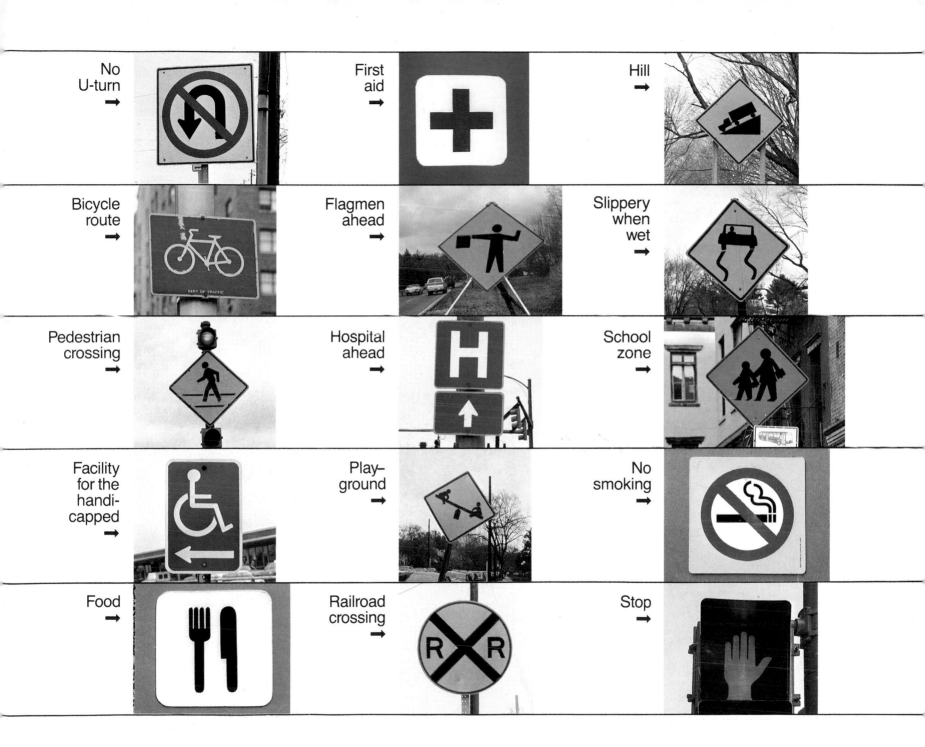

No U-turn ➡	First aid ➡	Hill ➡
Bicycle route ➡	Flagmen ahead ➡	Slippery when wet ➡
Pedestrian crossing ➡	Hospital ahead ➡	School zone ➡
Facility for the handi-capped ➡	Play-ground ➡	No smoking ➡
Food ➡	Railroad crossing ➡	Stop ➡

TANA HOBAN's photographs have been exhibited at the Museum of Modern Art in New York. She has won many gold medals and prizes for her work as a photographer and filmmaker. And, of course, her books for children are known and loved throughout the world.